If Big can run…
    … then I can run

(Though not as fast,
I'm only small)

If Big can jump…
… then I can jump

(And Big leaps long,
long, long away)

If Big can swing...

... then I can swing

(As Big swings
high into the sky,
I'll get there too,
one day, I'm sure)

If Big can climb...
...then I can climb

(It's just I have to take
my time to get to all the
places Big can climb to
with one stretch)

If Big can see...
...then I can saw

(Up, up I go, into the air.
I never thought I'd get so high,
but now that Big is on the ground
how will I get down?)

If Big can play...

...then I can play

(Deep in the sand Big digs a hole...

...but if I fell in I'd be stuck and then I'd have to yell and shout for Big to come and pull me out)

But what if Big
can't get in places
only I can squeeze inside?

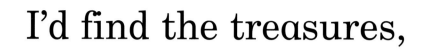

I'd find the treasures,

Rule the roost!

Be number one...

And Big would know
I'm having fun.

If Big could only see…

...how great it is
inside my den and all
the games I like to play
on oceans around the world
and spaceships in the sky.

Here I can
swing into
the air!

Running fast
and leaping long

and stretch to climb
and soaring high
into the air
and digging deep…

…but Big's not there…

...I'm all alone...

...and that's no fun,

so...

Whatever Big can...

and whatever I can...

We can…

...together!

For Danny, Beth, Mimi, and Joseph

B.S.

For Callum and Iain

P.B.

An Imprint of Sterling Publishing
387 Park Avenue South
New York, NY 10016

First published in this edition in 2006 by Meadowside Children's Books

This 2013 edition published by Sandy Creek.

ISBN 978-1-4351-4801-7

Manufactured in Guangzhou, China
Lot #:
2 4 6 8 10 9 7 5 3 1
05/13